KU-545-799

EGMONT
We bring stories to life

Christmas Angel first published in Great Britain 2002 by Egmont UK Limited
Santa's Reindeer first published in Great Britain 2002 by Egmont UK Limited
This edition published 2018 by Dean,
an imprint of Egmont UK Limited,
The Yellow Building, 1 Nicholas Road, London, W11 4AN
www.egmont.co.uk

Christmas Angel text by Laura Dollin
Christmas Angel illustrated by Rosalind Beardshaw

Santa's Reindeer text by Catherine Shoolbred
Santa's Reindeer illustrated by Liz Pichon

ISBN 978 0 6035 7576 1

70176/001

Printed in Malaysia

Christmas Angel *and* Santa's Reindeer

Christmas Angel

Look! Can you see me, glistening bright,

Right by the star on the Christmas tree?

Above every branch
and golden light
I'm the Christmas Angel,
for all to see.

On Christmas Eve, when everyone sings,
And stockings are hung at the end of your bed,

I fly, like magic, with golden wings
To wave some angel dust
over your head.

When the twinkling skies have gone away

And Christmas Day brings morning light,

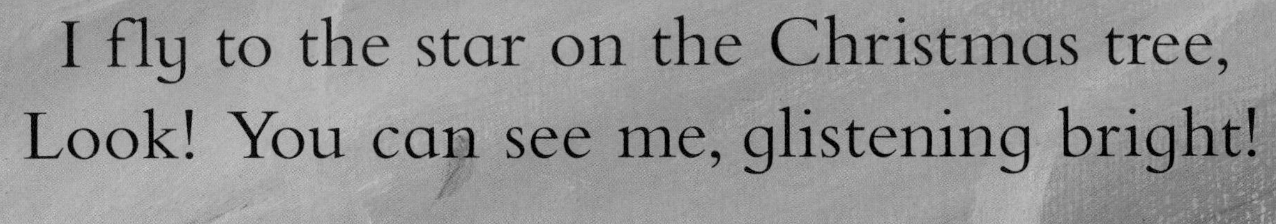

I fly to the star on the Christmas tree,
Look! You can see me, glistening bright!

Santa's Reindeer

It's Christmas time!

Santa's reindeer are very excited.

They watch Santa's helpers
carefully make all the toys.

They run races through the forest

to be fit for their long night.

And they eat lots of hay

to be strong for their flight.

They wait while the presents
are piled high on the sleigh.

Then they're off with Santa,
with the toys for Christmas Day!